an

The April Fools' Day Mystery

A Solve-It-Yourself Mystery

by Lucinda Landon

Secret Passage Press
Newport, Rhode Island

Books written & illustrated by Lucinda Landon:
Meg Mackintosh and...

The Case of the Missing Babe Ruth Baseball
The Case of the Curious Whale Watch
The Mystery at the Medieval Castle
The Mystery at Camp Creepy
The Mystery in the Locked Library
The Mystery at the Soccer Match
The Mystery on Main Street
The Stage Fright Secret
Solves Seven American History Mysteries
The Mystery at Red Herring Beach
The April Fools' Day Mystery

MegMackintosh.com

Library of Congress Cataloging-in-Publication Data

Landon, Lucinda.
    Meg Mackintosh and the April Fools' Day Mystery / a solve-it-yourself mystery / by Lucinda Landon. – 1st. ed.
    Summary: Meg Mackintosh's birthday is on April 1st, also known as April Fools' Day. Her celebration is interrupted by a curious message which sends her and her dog Skip off to solve a mystery. The reader may search the pictures for key clues to solve the case along with Meg.
    (1. Mystery and detective stories. 2. Literary recreations 3. April Fools' Day)

Library of Congress Control Number: 2017919837

ISBN 978-1-888695-15-1

10 9 8 7 6 5 4 3 2 1

PRINTED IN THE UNITED STATES OF AMERICA

In Memory of:
My Grandmother,
Mildred Martin Landon

"Meg-O!" Gramps called out. "Time for breakfast. We're all waiting." He glanced around Meg's room. "Where are you?"

Then Gramps noticed something coming down from the ceiling.

It was a yo-yo, with a message stuck on it!

The yo-yo rose back up into an opening between the beams where there was a trap door. A boot descended, followed by another. It was Meg. She carefully climbed down the bookcase from her secret hiding place.

"I thought you might be up there." Gramps gave her a hug. "Happy Birthday, Meg!"

"Thanks, Gramps. But wait a minute, I've got to get Skip." Meg grabbed a rope attached to a pulley and slowly lowered her dog down. Skip was secured in a little hammock.

"Very clever!" Gramps patted her on the back and they headed to the kitchen.

Her Mom and Dad sang out, "Happy Birthday to Meg!" Mom carried a stack of pancakes lit with candles.

Her brother Peter shouted, "Make a wish and blow out the candles!"

With a huge puff, Meg blew out all the candles. She tried to cut into the pancakes, but couldn't.

"These are rubber." Meg made a face. "I should have known."

"That's because it's your birthday and April Fools' Day!" They all laughed.

"Of course...my April Fools' birthday...ha, ha," Meg frowned. "Last year it was plastic cheese in my sandwich."

"Here are the real pancakes." Dad placed a new platter in front of her. "And look, lots of cards and presents!"

Meg smiled. "Hmm, presents. Are these real?"

"Yes, they're real," said Peter. "Well, maybe there are a few joke gifts. This one is from me."

Meg unwrapped Peter's gift. "This is definitely a joke!" She laughed.

"Now you can take a closer look at the clues when solving your next mystery," Peter said while everyone laughed.

"We can't help it you were born on April Fools' Day," said Dad.

"Why couldn't I have been born on March 31st or April 2nd?" Meg replied. She counted the candles as she pulled them out of the out of the pancakes.

"Only nine candles? Why am I still nine? I'm supposed to be ten! Really Mom and Dad, I feel like I've been nine forever." Meg gave them a serious look.

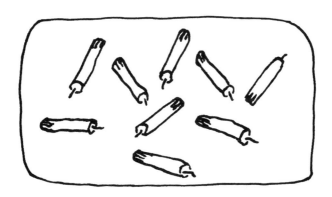

Mom and Dad looked at each other in shock. Gramps looked at the ceiling. Skip looked at Meg.

Then Peter blurted out, "It's because you're a character in a book! We all are. We don't get older!"

Mom and Dad held their breath.

Peter continued. "The author gave you your name and your birthdate. She made us all up, *even* Skip!"

"What?!?" Meg was very confused and angry.

"I don't believe you! I'm not a character! If this is another one of your jokes, it's not funny!"

Meg pushed away the presents and stood up.

"I'm tired of being nine and I'm tired of always being a detective. I want to do something else!"

No one knew what to say.

Gramps broke the silence. "But you're a great detective, and we love you just the way you are." He paused. "Maybe this will help. It's a letter for you." He handed it to Meg.

She opened it and read the message out loud.

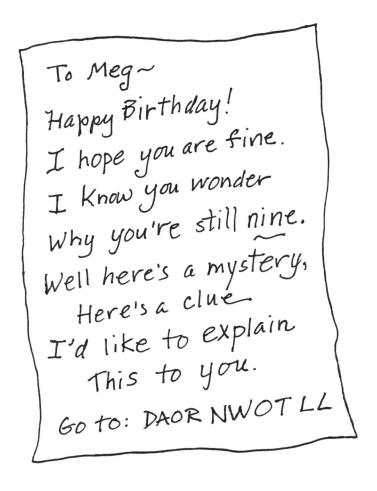

To Meg~
Happy Birthday!
I hope you are fine.
I know you wonder
why you're still nine.
Well here's a mystery,
Here's a clue
I'd like to explain
This to you.
Go to: DAOR NWOT LL

Meg asked, "Who sent this to me?"

Again, no one said a word.

A little annoyed, Meg said, "I guess I'll have to solve this one myself." She folded up the letter and stuck it in her pocket. Grabbing her detective knapsack, Meg checked to make sure she had all her equipment. "Everything's here — notebook, pen, magnifying glass, tweezers, camera, binoculars and flashlight."

Meg peered out the window. "Naturally, it's cloudy on my April Fools' birthday," she said putting on her Mackintosh raincoat. "Come on Skip, we're going to solve this mystery."

As they headed out the door, Meg looked back at her family and waved.

"Have fun cracking another case Meg-O," Gramps called out with a mischievous smile.

Peter proceeded to eat Meg's pancakes. "Is she really upset about being a character in a book? It's not that big of a deal," he said with his mouth full.

WHERE ARE MEG AND SKIP GOING?

When they were out of sight, Meg got out a pencil and her notebook and deciphered the clue.

"It looks like an address written backwards: *LL Town Road.*"

"An address usually begins with numbers not letters. Maybe whoever wrote the clue meant 77 Town Road. I know where that is," Meg told Skip. "It's a creepy old house, not far away. Everyone is scared to go there."

As they approached the driveway, Meg noticed that something was wrong with the old mailbox.

WHAT DOES MEG NOTICE?

"Now I get it," she said as she turned the numbers upright. "It looked like the letters *LL,* but it should be the number 77."

The mailbox door was hanging open. Meg peered inside and was surprised by what she saw!

It was a fake raven with a note in its beak. The note was hard to read because it had been burned around the edges.

"It looks like: *oorbel*," Meg deduced.

Meg got out her binoculars and peered at the house.

"Hmm…muddy footprints," she detected. Then Meg focused on something hanging on one of the doors.

"I think I know where we should go," she told Skip.

WHERE WOULD YOU GO?

The door on the right side of the house had old sleigh bells hanging on a nail.

"The letters *d* and *l* are missing in the burned clue. It should say *doorbell* and this is an old-fashioned doorbell!"

She ruffled Skip's ears and then they rang the bells. No one answered. But the door slowly creaked open.

"Come on Skip! We have to go in and investigate."

They stepped into the ancient house. Meg scanned the kitchen with her eyes. The ceiling was low and the floor sloped to one side. There was a stone sink with a funny faucet, and lots of old stuff on the counters and shelves.

"Hmm, now what do we do?" Meg thought out loud. Then she noticed something.

DO YOU SEE A CLUE IN THE KITCHEN?

Muddy footprints led to a pair of rubber boots. There was a piece of paper rolled up inside one of them. Meg uncurled it. It was a map. "Skip, it looks like a floor plan of this house."

She decided to follow the arrow through a doorway into the parlor.

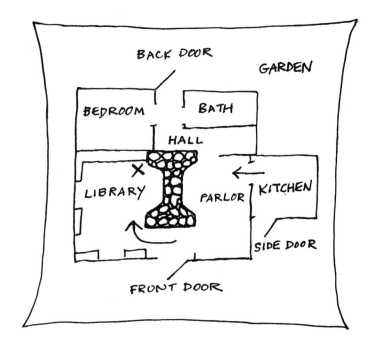

Meg noticed a faded photograph hanging on the wall. She examined it with her magnifying glass.

"Hmm, I do detect a bit of family resemblance," she joked. "And what a nice locket around the girl's neck."

In the parlor, two comfy chairs were set in front of the fireplace. Meg could still smell the burnt wood, but the fire was out. She dropped into one of the deep soft chairs, put her feet on a little stool, and glanced around.

Meg spoke to Skip in her fake British accent.
"Quite a mysterious place, old chap." But as she
reopened the map, her elbow accidently knocked an
old bowl off the table. If fell to the floor and
shattered into dozens of pieces.

"Oh, no! Now I've done it!" Meg ran to the
kitchen to find a dust pan and broom.

As Meg swept up, she realized that some of the chips of the china bowl had flown into the hearth. It was tricky getting them out of the deep ruts between the stones. Then she saw something glimmering between a hearthstone and a floorboard. She got her tweezers out of her knapsack and tried to grasp the shiny object.

After a few tries, she was able to grab it. She pulled it gently. It was a gold chain. Part of it was stuck under the wooden floorboard. Meg wiggled the old board, and the chain popped free. She rubbed away the dirt and realized it was the locket from the photo!

Then Meg noticed something on the side of the fireplace. She slipped the locket into her pocket and carefully leaned in to grab a small piece of paper tucked between the fireplace stones. "Skip, it's another clue!" Meg unfolded the note and read it:

What marks the spot?

DO YOU KNOW THE ANSWER?
WHERE WOULD YOU GO?

"Of course, X marks the spot!" She recalled seeing an X on the map. "We should go through this hallway near the front door."

They entered the next room. It was filled with books from floor to ceiling.

"Skip, we're in the library! Let's go to where the X is on the map."

Meg read the spines of the books. "A lot of my favorites." Then she noticed something peculiar.

DO YOU SEE ANYTHING UNUSUAL?

"Secret Passage Press." Meg paused. "Hmm, that's a bit odd. Why would there be a button on a book?"

She pressed the button. Suddenly, part of the bookshelf swung open to reveal a staircase.

"It's a real secret passage," Meg whispered. She turned on her flashlight and climbed the steep, narrow steps. Skip followed close behind.

At the top of the stairs was a dark hallway. Meg noticed a sliver of light coming from under a door. Slowly, she pushed the door open.

Meg squinted into the light. "Wow, a hidden artist's studio!" she whispered to herself.

She saw paints, canvases, and a large desk in front of a window.

Meg was shocked by what she saw next! A person slumped over the desk.

"Are you all right?" Meg shouted. "Oh no! Is that blood? Is everything okay?"

Suddenly, the figure sat up straight. "APRIL
FOOLS!!!" The woman called out.

"YIKES!!!" Meg screamed.

Both Meg and the woman froze for a second.

"I hope I didn't scare you too much!" the woman
said.

"Are you kidding? You really scared me! That's not
funny…not funny at all!" Meg shouted back. "I
thought that you were really hurt, I thought that was
real blood," Meg stared at the red puddle. "What is
it?"

"Only a little red paint," the woman said. "I'm
sorry I scared you. I just wanted to have some April
Fools' Day fun on your birthday."

"How do you know it's my birthday?" Meg asked her while pulling the letter out of her pocket. "Did you send this to me? Did you leave those clues?"

The woman bit her lip. "Well, yes, I did. It's hard to explain, but I've known you for a while."

Meg questioned her somewhat angrily, "How do you know me? My brother said somebody made me up! Was it you? How can that be?"

Before the woman could explain, Meg spotted a drawing of herself on the desk. The woman tried to cover it up. Not knowing what to say, the woman mumbled under her breath, "Oh dear, I thought this would be more fun."

"This is not fun for me," Meg frowned. "Why am I still nine years old? And why am I always solving mysteries?"

"Because that's who you are. You are a very, very smart detective." The woman tried to calm Meg. "Please don't get upset."

The woman fiddled with her pencil. "Meg, I am an author and an illustrator. Everything I make becomes real to me. You are very real."

"So," Meg paused, "You write and illustrate mystery stories about me *and* my dog?"

"Yes," the woman admitted, "I do."

Meg noticed an eraser on the desk. She grabbed it and started erasing herself. "Watch this! I'm erasing myself! What do you think of that?"

"OH NO!" shouted the woman. "Please don't do that! Please stop!"

Meg gave the woman a hard look…

"April Fools!!!" Meg shouted.

The woman's face went white.

Again, they both froze for a second.

"I think I got you back," Meg said with a grin.

"Yes, you did! You scared me!" The woman grabbed a pencil and drew Meg's arm back. "So you aren't really mad are you?" the woman asked.

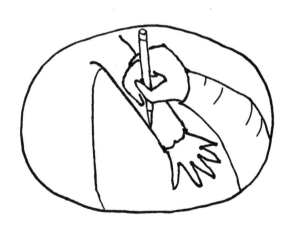

"I'm not mad, but I am confused," Meg replied.

"Well I can explain, but why don't we start with a truce?" the woman pleaded. "I don't think I can handle another prank."

"Yes," agreed Meg. "Truce."

"I think your pup would like some water," the woman suggested.

"His name is Skip," Meg said. "You should know that!"

"Of course...Skip," the woman said. She then took out an old bowl and poured water into it for the dog.

"That reminds me, I need to tell you something," Meg confessed.

WHAT DID MEG REMEMBER?

"I'm so sorry. I broke a bowl downstairs. It was an accident," Meg apologized. "I hope it wasn't some ancient artifact."

"Don't worry about it, I have plenty of old bowls," the woman replied.

"Oh, and when I was sweeping up I found something. It was wedged way down between a hearthstone and a floorboard. I cleaned it off a little."

Meg reached into her pocket and handed the locket to the woman.

"Oh my," the woman's eyes lit up. "My locket! I lost it years ago." The woman thanked Meg. "I can't believe you found it. See, you really are a great detective! Let me show you the picture inside."

"It's my first dog. Her name was Skye," the woman said as she opened the locket.

"She's adorable! And is that you in the photo in the parlor? Meg asked.

"Yes. My father took that picture of my mother and me on my tenth birthday," the woman replied.

"*LL*, those must be your initials." Meg said.

"Yes, but why don't you just call me *L*," she told Meg. "That's not too mysterious is it?"

"No, but speaking of names, why didn't you know Skip's name?" Meg questioned. "If we were made up characters, you would've known that. I want the truth. Remember, we agreed, no more pranks. Are Skip and I really made up characters?"

Why didn't **L** know Skip's name ?

WHAT DO YOU THINK?

"Of course I know Skip's name, but I don't know everything about you. I only write mysteries based on the stories I hear from Gramps," L confessed. "He was the one who set up this entire adventure."

"So, I'm not stuck at age nine? I can do more than solve mysteries forever? I'm not only a character in one of your books?" Meg questioned.

"No, no, no. This was all an April Fools' Mystery. And don't worry, that was the last one," explained L. "In fact, if you are tired of solving other people's mysteries, you should consider writing your own."

L picked something up from her desk. "This is for you. It's my *Mystery Writing Handbook*." L handed her the book. "It will help you get started brainstorming ideas."

"I think my brain has gone through enough storming today," Meg joked. "Thank you. This looks intriguing."

"Happy Birthday, Meg!" *L* gave her a hug. "And be sure to put some clues in your drawings."

"Absolutely," Meg replied, and she hugged *L* back. "It's been nice meeting you, but I think Skip and I should get going." Meg put the book in her knapsack.

"Of course," said *L*. "It's been wonderful to finally meet you in person!"

Meg climbed down the steep stairs of the secret passage. Skip was at her heels.

Once outside, Meg took a deep breath. "Well, that was pretty amazing." She rubbed Skip's head.

The wind had blown the 77 to look like *LL* again. Meg decided to leave it that way.

Gramps was waiting at a turn in the road. "How did it go?" he asked.

"Great!" replied Meg. "What a mysterious April Fools' Day. *L* is a *real character*," Meg laughed.

"Yes, she is," Gramps winked.

"Her house was creepy, but in a cool way," Meg added. "Like something out of a scary book. Maybe I'll write a mystery about it."

"Good idea," said Gramps. "I'm glad you had fun."

"I guess having a birthday on April Fools' Day isn't that bad after all," Meg grinned.

When they got home, Mom, Dad, and Peter were waiting for them. They had a birthday cake.

"Is that a real cake?" Meg asked, half joking.

"Yes," said her Mom. "A very, very real cake."

Meg blew out the candles and then counted them.

There were ten.

Get paper and pencils ready. Please do not draw in this book, (unless it is your own) and have fun!

What is a mystery?	Draw your detective
A mystery is a puzzle that a detective wants to solve. Clues give hints to how the mysterious event happened. The detective must find the clues, deduce what they mean, and put the pieces of the puzzle together, in order to solve the mystery.	

Draw a mysterious setting	Draw a detective kit

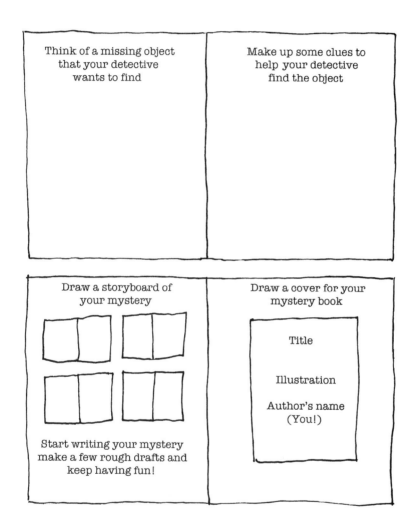

Think of a missing object
that your detective
wants to find

Make up some clues to
help your detective
find the object

Draw a storyboard of
your mystery

Start writing your mystery
make a few rough drafts and
keep having fun!

Draw a cover for your
mystery book

Title

Illustration

Author's name
(You!)

About the author

Lucinda Landon has always loved mysteries. She has also always loved to draw. After studying art at the Rhode Island School of Design, she illustrated *The Young Detective's Handbook*, by William Vivian Butler. That book received a special Edgar Allan Poe Award from the Mystery Writers of America and it launched Meg Mackintosh, who soon starred in her own adventures. The Meg Mackintosh Mystery series is now eleven books strong, all published by Secret Passage Press.

Lucinda Landon at age 10.
Photograph by her father, Ned Landon.

Learn more about Meg Mackintosh at:
MegMackintosh.com